HILLBILLY NIGHT AFORE CHRISTMAS

Hillbilly Night
Afore Christmas

Illustrated by JAMES RICE

Text by Thomas Noel Turner

PELICAN PUBLISHING COMPANY
Gretna 1994

Copyright © 1983
By James Rice and Thomas Noel Turner
All rights reserved

First printing, 1983
Second printing, 1991
Third printing, 1994

The word "Pelican" and the depiction of a pelican are trademarks
of Pelican Publishing Company, Inc., and are registered
in the U.S. Patent and Trademark Office.

Library of Congress Cataloging in Publication Data

Turner, Thomas Noel.
  Hillbilly night before Christmas.

  Adaptation of: Night before Christmas / Clement
Clarke Moore.
  Summary: An adaptation in mountain dialect of the
well-known poem about an important Christmas visitor.
  1. Children's poetry, American. 2. Christmas—
Juvenile poetry. 3. Santa Claus—Juvenile poetry.
[1. Santa Claus—Poetry. 2. Christmas—Poetry.
3. American poetry. 4. Narrative poetry] I. Rice,
James, 1934   , ill. II. Moore, Clement Clarke,
1779-1863. Night before Christmas. III. Title.
PS3570.U735H5   1983   811'.54   83-4120

ISBN 0-88289-367-X

Manufactured in Hong Kong

Published by Pelican Publishing Company, Inc.
1101 Monroe Street, Gretna, Louisiana 70053

'Twas the night afore Christmas
    'Twixt ridgeback and holler,
No critter was twitchin'
    Nary hawg dast to waller.

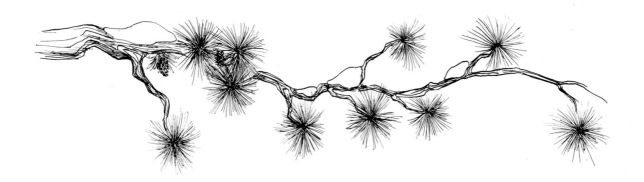

Each keerful darn't stockin'
    War' nail't near the chimbley,
A hopin' that Sainty'd
    Be a extry bit fren'ly.

The youngun's was snuggle't
Grub deep in the tickin',
Dream conjurin' up or'nges
And stripe't candy lickin'.

Ole Maw in her night dress
     And me in my long johns,
Wuz a snorin' es happy
     Es frogs in thuh lake ponds.

When up in the piney woods
    Come a scair't paint'er screechin',
Ain't heered sich a ruckus
    Since camp meetin' preachin'.

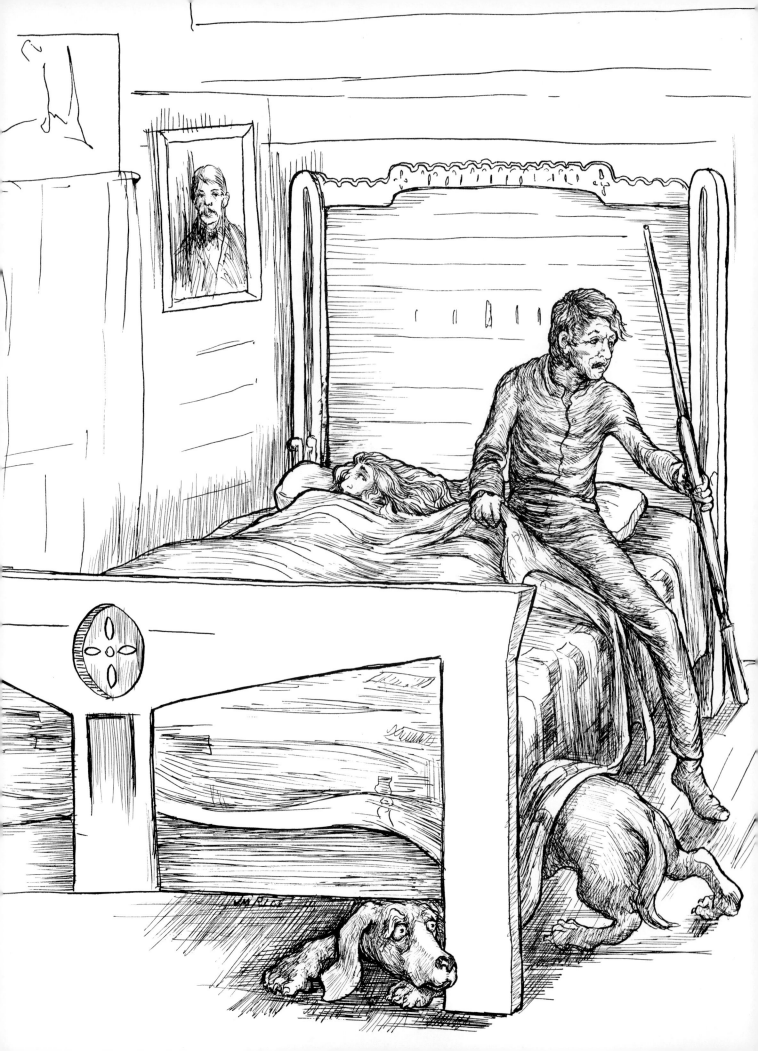

Wuz thet wu'thless houn', Blue,
    With a growl full of shiver,
Tried tuh crawl 'neath thuh bedstid,
    I th'owed off thuh kivver.

I grabb't fer my rifle gun,
    'Most farred hit off too,
Then tremblin' in sock feet
    Near tripp't on ole Blue.

Aire plank door creaked dreadful
    Jist op'nin' a mite,
So's I knowed flat out sartin
    Ha'nts walked th'ew thuh night.

They's a bright punkin' moon
    Tuh bring moonshiners sorrah,
Made it middle day brightness
    Like thuh woods wuz a-far.

Kindly dreamy, way yonder,
    Pure floatin' up aire,
Come a ole timey wagon
    And eight smokey bear.

With a sawed off ole peddler
    As quick as a bainty,
Hit whomped like a mule kick,
    Thet had to be Sainty.

To beat hummin' birds' wings
    Thet bear passel came,
Whilst he growled, "Gee!" then "Haw!"
    Es he hollered the'r names.

"On, Big Feet! On, Orn'ry!
　　"Molasses an' Rumbler!
"Up, Yowler! Up, Growler!
　　"On, Gumption an' Grumbler!"

"Git over thet hinhouse!
　　"Light out to the shed!
"Now climb, you ole honey bears!
　　"Jist mind what I said!"

Es biddies fum sarpents
　　Ur Maw's stripe't cat,
Fluster which way to go,
　　Firstly this'n, then that.

So's up to the tin roof
　　Them spry varmints clumb,
With a good few of purties
　　And ole Sainty, by gum.

And d'recly I heered
     Sich a turrible trompin',
Like'n hail big es bisquit bread,
     Ur store teeth a chompin'.

Though I near met myself,
     Tarn'ed quick es a toad,
Sainty skinned down that chimbley
     'Fore I ever knowed.

He wuz snortin' and fussin',
     Stompin' snow fum his feet,
Breshin' off suht leavin's
     Whut stuck tuh his seat.

He'd a mouth made fer smiles
  Twicet too big fer elf-size,
A red jelly bean nose
  An' shoe button eyes.

His britches and coat,
  Wuz pure worryation,
Of quiltin' piece patches
  Tuh beat all creation.

He wore 'spenders and belt
  Like a man wif' a callin',
Tuh persactly be sartain
  His paints wuzn't fallin'.

You could tell he liked vittles
  Like stack cake and spoon bread,
An' al'ays tuk seconts
  When seconts wuz fed.

He'd granpappy whiskers,
    But his twinkledy eyes
Made him look like a youngun
    Whose smile never lies.

He looked plumb full of happy,
    Bof' cheeks puff't out wide,
Like a chaw of terbacky
    Wuz helt in each side.

A burn't black ole corn cob
    He 'peared 'bout to swaller,
Ever which way he goed
    Thuh smoke seem't tuh foller.

He'd shouldered a tote
    Stuffed to make yur eyes shine,
Made him out sum ole trapper
    A-tendin' his line.

He squinched up one eye,
    Give a "How d'ye do" grin,
Not a orphin nur widder
    Coulda been ascairt then.

He wuz more do than talk,
    To his chores bent his back,
Stuffed them stockin's right quick
    An' then heffed that there sack.

Then a pintin' me hush
    'Til my "Set a spell" friz,
With a meetin' house nod
    Out'n thuh chimbley he riz.

To his wagon he scrambled
    Real squirrely an' spritely,
Whupped them ole bears
    Kinda soft an' perlitely.

They lit out a bellerin'
    Like scairt scalded pups,
Ole Sainty, red wagon,
    An' smokey bear cubs.

But I give him a holler
   Afore he got clear,
"Merry Christmas, ole boy,
   "Y'all come back, yuh hear!"